I0727119

Fang:
An Alien Scifi Romance

DEMELZA CARLTON

ONE

"So what are the aliens like?" Dani demanded eagerly.

Flora rolled her eyes. "The same as they were when you asked last week, or the week before. Mostly, they look like us. Just people. But some of them have different coloured skin, or horns, or fur, or scales, or you can see through them.

Once I saw on the news this rescue worker just poofed out of nowhere, grabbed someone out of the crashed aircar, and then poof, they disappeared again. So at least one of them can teleport."

"I wish one would teleport in here, so we could meet him!" Dani said.

Flora and Linnaea just shook their heads. "No, you don't. This is our little enclave, where we're safe. Out there in the city, anything could happen. I mean, it wasn't too long ago that we were at war with the aliens, and the Watch break up fights every night. If aliens knew about us and this place, they'd teleport in here and kidnap you in a flash, a slave to their alien desires, and no one would ever see you again."

"It can't be any worse than farm work," Dani said. "I mean, you'd spend all day in bed, and hardly wear any clothes so you wouldn't need to do as much laundry. You might even get better food than protein bars." She eyed hers with distaste. Maybe if they tasted better, or weren't so hard to chew, she'd manage to choke one down, but right now…she couldn't even make herself do that.

"Fewer clothes to wash, but way more bed linen. Definitely not less laundry," Iva said.

She'd been raised in the brothel where her mother worked, back on Earth, Dani knew, though Iva rarely talked about her childhood. She'd heard whispers that Iva had actually worked in the brothel, though she couldn't have been more than fifteen when she left that place to join the FarmStar program. She and Flora had been the poster girls on the ads Dani had seen, which had made her want to sign up.

A year of learning intensive terraforming and farming techniques, before they'd been packed off to the *Genesis* to be put into stasis, where they'd remained until they woke up on Star Farm, their own corner of the Colony, until Donna could make arrangements for a planetside land grant where they could start farming properly.

So with the colonising part of their contract on hold for the moment, Donna had decided to bring forward the breeding part. They'd all signed on, knowing they'd need to work for a number of years and bear children for the Colony, but Dani had thought that meant human babies, not alien ones.

She eyed Linnaea's swelling belly. She was the first pregnant girl among them, though not for long, according to Donna.

"What's it like to…you know…make babies with an alien?" Dani asked.

Flora snorted. "The same as with a human, of course. He puts his penis in the right place, pumps a few times, and makes a baby. Or weren't you paying attention in sex ed class?"

"That was back on Earth. Before we knew we'd be having sex with aliens. So, what was his…you know…like?"

Linnaea shrugged. "I don't know."

Dani gaped. "What do you mean you don't know? He did stick it into you, didn't he? Or was it all probes and things while you were unconscious?"

Flora smacked her hand. "Dani! Where do you get these ideas from?"

Dani shrugged. "The TV was always on at the orphanage, playing all sorts of things. Sometimes, late at night, there were programs about aliens that really weren't suitable for kids. I used to sneak out and watch them. There were scary aliens, friendly aliens, and sexy aliens. So which one was the father of your baby, Linnaea?"

Linnaea huffed out an impatient breath. "I don't know, all right? It was dark, he bent me over a table, it was painful but at least it was quick, and then he was gone. Three weeks later, on my weekly health check, the scanner said I was pregnant, and…that's it. I don't want to talk about it, okay?"

But Dani just couldn't let it drop. "But in sex ed class we were always told that it would be painful at first, but then it would become pleasurable. Didn't you enjoy it at all?"

"No. Maybe he was too quick, so we didn't get to the good part. What's it matter? In a few months, I'll give birth to the first baby I'm contracted to carry for the Colony, and I'll only have to breed with an alien three more times before my body is my own."

"Yeah, but…the same alien, or a different one? Maybe the next one you get will be better at giving pleasure.

Maybe he'll want you to carry all his babies. Or maybe you'll get to try out four different aliens, and choose the one you like best. Or…"

"Enough, Dani. It's time to start work. Quick, finish your breakfast before Donna notices. She's coming over here!" Flora rose to her feet, offering a hand to help Linnaea up. She frowned at Rue, who was already halfway across the field with the best seeder. "Suck up," she muttered.

"She's not, honestly. Rue just likes farming more than people," Dani said.

Linnaea sniffed. "Yeah, but she makes the rest of us look bad for not being so eager to get started. At least I have an excuse for being slow now." She patted her belly.

Dani reluctantly rose, and started to follow the others toward the equipment shed.

"Dandelion, stop! You are to report to the medical room for a health check. You haven't eaten in two days, which is unacceptable. The health of Star Farm depends on you staying healthy, or you'll let everyone down. You don't want to do that, do you?"

For a moment, she considered lying and saying she didn't care. Or that she couldn't eat because she was too excited about meeting aliens for the first time. But the first would land her in solitary for a week, and the second would see someone else take her place. So she simply lowered her head and said, "No, Donna. I hope a health check will tell me how to do better."

"Good girl." Donna patted her shoulder, then followed close behind her all the way up to the medical room.

TWO

"Come on…put the thing on the thing, and be done with it!" Talon begged.

Claw sniffed, then delicately picked up one of the white tiles and held it over the go board, oscillating between one indentation and another. Finally, he deposited it somewhere else entirely.

"Wait…what?" Talon cried.

Claw shrugged. "If you paid more attention to the game instead of insisting that I play faster, one day you might actually be able to beat me."

"I beat you last time — and Achilles, too! I was last month's champion!" Talon insisted. "Back me up here, Fang."

Fang sighed and put down his tablet. The rules of go night included, among other things, no work. A rule he usually managed to obey, because his patients never came with him. But an emergency message from one of his courier ships, asking permission to answer a distress call from a mining ship wasn't something he got every day, and it wasn't something that could wait, either. "Sorry, I had to authorise a response to a distress call."

Claw frowned. "Why? Under the Altan

System Treaty, all ships have to respond to an emergency distress call. Don't tell me your ships are doing something illegal, Fang."

"It's not a normal distress call. The mining ship isn't in trouble. They've found…wreckage, and emergency pods, and they're asking for help to transport the pods to a facility that can get the people out of them. The question isn't whether they should offer to help, but who's paying, while my ships are contracted to the courier company. The courier company isn't responding, which means they don't want to pay, so he contacted me. My captains know it's company policy to take the cost of a delay out of their salary and bonuses, and this will be a big detour. But our cargo holds are much safer than the ones on the mining ship. So no, Claw, unless it's become illegal to go and save people, I and my ships are not doing anything illegal, that I know of. Not that you should care, anyway. It's not like you're writing laws any more, or trying to convict people who break them."

"I definitely prefer baking to lawbreaking, but you're my friend, so if you needed legal advice, I might be willing to leave my nice, quiet retirement to do a friend a favour," Claw said.

"Just as long as you'll still bring your bear claws to our next go night," Talon said, lifting the last pastry in a toast to its baker, before devouring it in three bites. The griffon shifter might look like a human now, but he always gulped his food like a griffon.

Claw's hands sprouted claws, which he flexed for a moment before they disappeared. "I always bring my bear claws." He reached over and placed another tile on the go board. "And I believe I win."

Talon swore, Fang laughed, and Claw folded his arms across his chest with a smug little smile.

"And as my winnings, I'm going to ask the two of you for a favour."

This, too, was part of the rules of go night. The night's champion could ask whatever he would of the others, though usually he just ended up not paying for his food and drink that night, while the others chipped in to cover the costs.

"I'm going to a speed dating event on

Friday night, and I want you both to come with me as my wingmen," Claw said.

"What?" Talon exploded.

Fang just shook his head. "I don't date. I definitely don't speed date. And all the speed dating events I've seen around are trying to matchmake Humans with Titans to cash in on the mixed race baby bonus. Human girls run screaming when they hear I'm a vampire, and we all know vampires aren't much use for breeding purposes."

"But where do little vampires come from?" Talon asked.

Fang shot him a dirty look. As if Talon didn't already know. "The same place your mother pushed you out of. Only vampire couples aren't fertile unless they're fated mates, and properly mated, and even then they're lucky to even have one kid, if they have any at all." He couldn't remember the last time he'd heard of a new vampire mating. Not since they'd arrived in the Altan System, that was for sure.

"Then you have to go along! What if your fated mate is waiting at the Agency for you?" Talon teased.

"Don't griffons mate for life, too? What if you have a fated mate, and she's going to be at this event?" Fang shot back.

Claw patted the air. "Guys, guys! If either of you meet the love of your life, I will totally stand aside and excuse you from wingman duties for the night. Who knows what could happen at these things? I just need you both to go with me. I'll even pay for your tickets, food and drink. How's that?"

Talon perked up. "Is this the one they do at Forge?" Fang could already see Talon's mind working on the possibilities of racking up a huge bill on Claw's tab.

"No, it's at the First Shot Cantina. The dating agency that meets at Forge is run by cupids, and it's all about looking for love, not specifically matching Humans with Titans. This one's…more for people interested in breeding."

"So the food and drink will be shit, but the chances of getting laid are super high," Talon translated.

"For you, maybe. I'm still a vampire," Fang said.

Talon clapped him on the back.

"Yeah, but you're a rich, hot vampire dentist. I'm sure Human girls really go for that."

Fang snorted. "Yeah, like they love guys who spend so long in animal form they forget how to use a fork." He shuddered at the mess Talon was making with his pasta. Griffons were gross.

"So it's a deal, yes? All three of us, going speed dating at the First Shot Cantina next Friday night. I'll send you the time and other details to your tablets. Do not be late." Claw said, draining the last of his drink. "I have bread to knead, so it'll rise in time for tomorrow, and my pastries won't make themselves." With a final wave, he was gone.

"You have time for another drink, or are you leaving, too?" Talon asked, turning to Fang.

Fang checked the time. "I have all night to get home, and no more patients tonight. I could manage another drink, if you have the good stuff."

Talon grinned. "Well, what do you know? I got my hands on a bottle of genuine Earth-brewed tequila from Eden this week, as thanks for my pest control services. All those years at university, studying animals, when my real talents were in telling the meowls what to do while I sit back and let them do all the work."

"Yeah, but that's only because you bred superior meowls in the first place, which you couldn't have done without those years of study. And the fact that you bred them in space on the *Titanic*, and invited us up for a go night there the very same night Titania went mad and all hell broke lose, which saved all our lives and most of your breeding stock…"

Talon pulled the stopper out of the bottle, then glugged the contents into two glasses. He raised his glass, and nodded for Fang to do the same. "To meowls, miracles and fate that loves us," he said.

"Meowls, miracles, and fate's favour," Fang agreed, knocking his back. Yep, he still hated tequila. Give him a healthy bottle of blood any time. Or a bitter, rich coffee liqueur. Next time, when it was his turn to host, perhaps.

"So, any idea why Claw would want to go to some matchmaking event for breeders?" Talon asked.

Fang just shook his head. "Maybe he thinks his biological clock is ticking. Or maybe…maybe he's doing this as a favour for someone, too, and taking us along so he doesn't look suspicious. I mean, you'll draw all the attention, so no one will notice him or me."

Talon burst out laughing. "Yeah, right up until the Human girls realise griffon babies are born in a litter of at least three. Then they run screaming from me, too."

"Let's face it, we're all doomed to remain lifelong bachelors. Achilles, too."

"Well, yeah, but he's…you know."

Fang nodded. "Yeah. Makes griffon quintuplets sound easy."

"I was only a triplet, you know. There might not be more than three."

Fang sobered. "That's three more kids than I'll ever have." Not that he'd planned on having any, given the odds on it ever happening, but sometimes he imagined…

He poured two more glasses of tequila. "To being lifelong bachelors," he said solemnly.

"Two lonely old men," Talon said glumly.

Fang wasn't sure whether to drink to that, or call it a night. So he did both, wiping his mouth with the back of his hand before waving farewell as he ventured out into the perpetual night that wreathed the Nyx Dome of the Colony where they lived.

THREE

"Strip."

Dani was already pulling her dress over her head before she heard the command, and she lay down on the examining table before Donna could ask her to do that, either. A moment later, Donna had the hand scanner switched on, and began the first pass down Dani's body. She prayed that it wouldn't find anything except a mouth ulcer, for which she'd have to take extra vitamins, but that was it.

God, but it was cold in the medical room. Her nipples felt like hard chips of ice and there was an annoying draft that wanted to waft right up between her legs and inside her, but if she closed her legs, Donna would only tell her to open them slightly again, and if you gave the air in the room an inch, it was right back in there, chilling her flesh like some sort of randy ice alien.

Ooh, were there ice aliens? Flora and Linnaea hadn't mentioned them, but just because they hadn't seen them didn't mean they didn't exist. There could be dozens of different aliens the other girls didn't even know about — and some of them might even be looking for love at the dating agency event she was finally going to be allowed to go to.

The scanner beeped to indicate it had finished its assessment. Dani sat up, curious to see what the readout looked like. Thankfully, Donna didn't pull it away, out of view this time.

"What is it?" Dani asked.

Donna's frown deepened. "This says your wisdom teeth need to be removed."

Dani's heart sank. "You can do that right here, right?" Donna was a capable nurse and a medic. She could handle most things.

"Of course not. You'll need to go to a dentist for this procedure. Right away, if you're to be fit and healthy in time to attend the speed dating event." Donna pulled out her tablet and began tapping at the screen. "Right, I've arranged the next available appointment for you at nine with a dental clinic in Metropolis City. You can go in a skimmer, and then come right back."

"But it's already nine thirty," Dani protested. "I can't possibly be there in time. Plus, we have to finish planting Field Six today, and – "

"You have a dentist appointment tonight at 9pm. Plenty of time to finish planting that field, before you go see the dentist, and then come straight back home for a good night's sleep before a full day's work tomorrow."

Oh God. No. Not the dentist. "That can't be right. Dentists don't work that late at night. It must be a mistake."

"This one's a vampire, and he does. No more excuses. Your health is our primary concern, and I will not let you neglect it a moment longer. Now, back to work to finish that field before your appointment."

"Yes, Donna," Dani said meekly as she pulled her clothes back on.

A vampire dentist. She wasn't sure which scared her more…except that if he was a vampire, then he was also an alien, because the only vampires in the Colony were Titans. She wasn't sure which scared her more – that he was an alien, that he was a vampire, or that he was a dentist.

She closed her eyes, not wanting to admit it.

Aliens she could handle, even if they hurt her like Linnaea's had. Vampires…she'd only heard stories about them, and never actually met one, so she was about as curious as she was scared of meeting a vampire. But a dentist…ever since she was a little girl, nothing terrified her more than a visit to the dentist.

If her mouth didn't hurt so much…

If Donna hadn't ordered her to go…

If her first speed dating event wasn't so close, and she hadn't been looking forward to it, well, since forever…or at least since she'd first heard about it, and she'd only be allowed to go if she was in perfect health…

Dani blew out a breath as she slipped on her shoes. Fine. She'd be brave and go to the dentist, no matter how much he scared her, and she'd have those unnecessary teeth removed, just like Donna wanted her to. But she didn't have to like it.

FOUR

Fang looked at his schedule. Last appointment of the night – a wisdom teeth extraction. Hang on, that couldn't be right – he always had his assistant book an anaesthetist well in advance for those, because the mild pain relief he offered wasn't always enough when an extraction turned nasty, which they did, more often than not. How could Elisa have let this booking be made without making the necessary arrangements?

A few minutes of fighting the booking system, and he had his answer. The appointment had only been booked today – Elisa mustn't have seen it before she left.

Well, he'd do a quick examination on…Dandelion, or that's what the booking system said her name was, and schedule another appointment to do the extraction when he could get an anaesthetist into the clinic.

"Dandelion?" he called, walking into the waiting room.

"Yes?" The voice was breathless with fear, almost drowned out by her thrumming heartbeat.

Definitely not doing this extraction tonight. Maybe not at all. Fang held up his hands. "It's all right, you don't need to be afraid. I can reschedule your appointment with my Human colleague in a few days' time."

She shook her head, and threads of gold parted from her plait, giving her a halo. "It won't matter. He'll still be a…"

"He's as Human as Human can be, I promise. Not a vampire at all," Fang said.

She swallowed, opening her golden brown eyes wide. "But he'll still be a dentist," she said softly.

Realisation dawned. "You're afraid of dentists?"

This small, shivering Human girl pressed her lips together and nodded.

"I need my wisdom teeth extracted, and only a dentist can do it," she said. She rose, lifting her chin with the kind of determination Fang couldn't help but admire. "Let's do this."

Fang knew better than to stand in the way of that kind of determination. He gestured toward the treatment room, "This way."

Her heart rate didn't slow as she took her place in the chair, or as he lifted up the scanner to take some preliminary images before he even asked her to open her mouth.

One look and he knew why she was here, fear of dentists or not.

"This one's impinging on the nerve. It must really hurt. And this one…have you been experiencing bad headaches lately?"

Dandelion nodded. "Will the headaches go away once you take my wisdom teeth out?"

He hesitated. They might, if he managed to stay away from that nerve during surgery, but depending on how deep he had to go, he still might leave it partially exposed, which meant the headaches might even get worse. But she was waiting for an answer. "Maybe."

She seemed satisfied with this. "And will I be able to eat again without my teeth hurting?"

"Oh, easily. Tomorrow, even, as long as you're careful. Nothing too hot or too cold or too hard…"

"Protein bars."

Fang nodded. "Those should be safe,

if a bit tasteless."

Wait, was that a smile?

"I didn't know vampires ate ration bars."

If she'd been a Titan, she'd know it was rude to ask about a Titan's strengths and weaknesses. But most Titans knew vampires didn't just survive on blood, and they wouldn't have to ask, like this innocent Human was.

Fang sighed. "Not willingly, but when needs must, I have managed to force one down. Actually, a vampire's diet is very similar to what most Humans eat, with the addition of a requirement for fresh blood and, of course, as little sunlight as possible."

"I'm sorry, I didn't know that. I've never met a vampire before."

He nodded. "Now, open your mouth so I can examine you, please." He flicked on the light.

She squeezed her eyes shut and opened her mouth wide.

Now if only she wasn't digging her nails so deeply into the arms of the chair…

A quick glance only confirmed what the images had told him. "Those need to come out."

She nodded. "Yes. Do it. Right now."

He grimaced. "The only thing is…it might hurt. I usually bring in an anaesthetist for extractions, because she's licenced to use stronger stuff than what I have at my disposal. I mean, my venom might be enough, but it might take more than one shot of it over the course of the procedure. And…"

Her eyes flew open. "Did you say venom?"

FIVE

When the alien vampire dentist explained it, it didn't sound all that bad. The venom he injected when he bit people had an anaesthetic effect. Venom applied to a wound site could also accelerate healing, so instead of recovery taking a week or more, her incisions could heal overnight. He only took a small sip of blood while waiting for the full dose of venom to be injected – only a spoonful, really, and he always healed the bite marks with a lick of venom so there would be no trace.

"Show me," she said, barely aware she was going to say the words before they were out, too late to take back.

"Are you sure?"

He looked so worried, like he feared for her. As if she wasn't already scared enough. What more did she have to be afraid of?

"Bite me," she hissed.

And he did.

A tiny sting at first as his sharp teeth pierced the skin at her neck, before what must have been his venom trickled through her veins, a cold prickling that lasted for only a moment before it was over, the venom swept away into her bloodstream. The rasp of his tongue along the side of her neck made her freeze, and then it was gone.

"Just healing the bite mark. Nothing inappropriate, I promise," the vampire said as he moved to stand in front of her, pulling his mask back into place. "How do you feel?"

"My…teeth don't hurt any more," she said slowly. Then the venom hit her, like she'd injected a whole bottle of champagne into her bloodstream. Was that what an orgasm felt like? The edge of her vision grew fuzzy, so all she could focus on was the vampire's face.

"Do it. Just you. I trust you," she said.

As she stared dreamily up into his kind

eyes, which were all she could see of his face over the mask, she was surprised to realise it was true. Even if he was a dentist.

An eternity passed, thought it seemed like only a moment, while she was lost in his eyes.

Then he said, "All done."

Wait…what?

SIX

When she said, "Bite me," Fang knew he was lost. He leaned in, breathing her clean scent, pressed his lips to her soft throat, and slid his teeth into the vein. Just the tip, so he only had a taste, while flooding her with venom, before he forced himself to withdraw. He allowed himself the pleasure of licking her neck, cleaning away blood and bite marks, before he swallowed.

If he'd thought he was lost before…stars, that one tiny taste obliterated him. He literally saw stars and nothing else. It was better than an orgasm. Better than a dozen orgasms, all piled up on top of each other. When he could finally see again, he moved to stand in front of her, where he could see if he'd had the same effect on her as she'd had on him.

No, surely she wouldn't look so calm and collected if he'd just given her a dozen orgasms. She'd be flushed, feverish, her lips parted and her eyes bright as she panted, begging for more just like he wanted to.

"How do you feel?" he asked. It came

out sounding clinical and professional. Not like he'd pitched a tent in his pants at all, even as he willed his erection to go down.

She looked thoughtful for a moment before she told him her teeth didn't hurt any more.

Perhaps now he could send her away, so she could return for another appointment when there was an anaesthetist present and he wouldn't have to bite her again. Because if he did, he was afraid he'd lose control.

"Do it. Just you. I trust you," she said.

Her golden brown eyes glowed with sincerity. With belief. He could do this, and earn the trust she was offering him.

He forced himself to focus, wielding the tools of his trade with vampire swiftness, but he wasn't fast enough. When she hissed in pain, he was forced to remove his mask and bite her again. Just the tip, he told himself, to take as little as possible, but even those few drops burned him like fire, unable to stop himself pitching a tent again.

Finally, the surgery was finished, but he had one more trick he'd promised to perform for her. "Close your eyes, so that I can heal the incisions," he said.

Obediently, her eyes drifted shut.

Normally, he'd drip a little venom onto his gloved fingers and rub it along the wounds. But he wanted to give this brave girl more than a few drops. He wanted to heal her completely, if he could. Venom pooled on his tongue as he hesitated. Then he struck.

He leaned in, pressing his lips to her open mouth, and swept his venom-coated tongue around her mouth, following the taste of blood until there was none left. Not a trace of blood or any sign that she'd had surgery.

He longed to keep kissing her, but he knew he could not. Instead, he forced himself to straighten and take a step back. "All done," he said, wishing it were not true. He'd done the best work of his career…but he could never tell anyone, because he could lose his job over that one kiss.

She winced as she sat up, feeling her face.

More than ever, he wished there was an anaesthetist here to help with her pain.

"Does it hurt?" he asked.

She bit her lip and nodded.

"I will give you a prescription that you can take to the pharmacy, some pain relief that should help over the next few days, but as they're closed now and won't be open until morning, would you like another shot of venom to tide you over until then?" he asked.

Again, she nodded.

He leaned in, not daring to touch her any more than necessary, but her scent was intoxicating now, as if the more time he spent with her, the more drunk he became.

"Just a tiny prick," he whispered, more to himself than to her, before he pierced her again. A full shot of venom, then a second, he pumped into her, willing it to be enough to tide her over until morning, before he added a third, unable to bear the thought of her in pain because of anything he'd done.

Then he pulled away, rushing to stand behind the reception desk before she could see his rock hard cock trying to escape his pants to impale her. He swallowed, forgetting that he had a mouthful of her blood.

The stars appeared for only a moment, before they went nova. Oh, stars…Fang had to grip the reception desk with both hands to stay upright as a hundred, or maybe a thousand orgasms, seemed to hit him all at once and…

Well, that was one way to end an erection, even if he now needed clean scrubs.

SEVEN

Dani daydreamed for the whole skimmer ride back to Star Farm, as well as Donna's scan in the medical room, which now claimed she was a picture of health. She crept into the dormitory, having to feel around for her bunk so as not to wake anyone by turning on the light.

Then she fell into bed and possibly the best dreams she'd ever known.

Because in her dreams, she wasn't alone in bed. Instead, she shared the sheets with a lover who wanted to kiss her everywhere, all at once, and in the dream he could, until the tingles all over her body had her panting, begging for more than just his lips.

And her dream lover gave it to her. There was no pain, unlike Linnaea's clumsy lover, only pleasure that went on and on and on.

Through all of it, all she could see of him was his eyes in the dark. Kind eyes, above a mask.

In the morning, the other girls asked where she'd been, and she told them she'd had a dentist's appointment. She received a few sympathetic nods, but no questions, thank goodness.

At breakfast, the dining room was filled with excited chatter about the upcoming speed dating event. That was tonight? She'd completely forgotten about it, too wrapped up in fantasies about the alien vampire dentist with the kind eyes.

This was exactly what she needed. An alien lover to chase all thoughts of the dentist out of her head. It wasn't like she could date a dentist, no matter how kind he might be.

But if another alien vampire turned up…she might happily tell him to bite her.

EIGHT

Fang cleaned himself up, then returned to his desk to write up Dandelion's notes. He'd forgotten to tell her to make a follow up appointment, just to be sure everything was healing properly and she wasn't experiencing any negative aftereffects, so he shot a message to the comm listed under her booking, only to find it answered by an older woman who looked nothing like Dandelion.

"Star Farm, this is Donna," the woman said.

"I was looking to speak to Dandelion, please," he said.

"Dandelion is a member of the Star Farm Collective. All communications pass through reception, before they are forwarded through to the relevant member of the Collective," she said. "Please state your message."

"I…Dandelion needs to make a follow up appointment. I'm her dentist," Fang said.

Donna squinted at the screen, as if staring at something other than Fang. "How soon?"

Tomorrow, he wanted to say, but he'd

promised to attend the dating thing with Claw tomorrow. "In two or three days' time," he said instead.

"How about 9pm in two days?" Donna asked.

"That would be perfect," Fang said.

"Then you will see her then." The call ended, leaving Fang staring at a blank screen.

He did not like that woman. Especially when she prevented him from speaking to Dandelion.

Suspicion prickled the back of his neck, so he typed STAR FARM COLLECTIVE into his tablet and hit SEARCH.

It was listed under the directory of all Colony businesses, as an all-women farming collective formed on Earth to terraform Elysium. Unusually, the women of the Star Farm Collective, under its original name of FarmStars, had been some of the original colonists actually selected for the Altan System. They'd volunteered and been selected for the colony, and had gone into early stasis aboard the *Genesis* before cargo was loaded. Unlike most of the Humans now living here, who'd climbed aboard the vessel to escape the destroyed space station where the ship was being constructed.

She must have been very important back on Earth, to have been loaded onto the ship first, when so few of the selected colonists had made it aboard. Likely some rich man's daughter, which explained why she had a bulldog of a secretary like Donna to make her appointments for her, and monitor her communications. Dandelion's father likely didn't think a dentist worthy of even looking at his daughter, let alone talking to her.

Maybe the man was right. After all, Fang only had his dental practice, and a small fleet of courier ships to his name. Hardly enough to impress a princess who'd been promised Elysium.

It was a good thing he'd agreed to go to that dating thing with Claw and Talon, he decided. Maybe he would go in, hoping for a hookup. Someone who could banish Princess Dandelion and her mindblowing blood from his mind. Best to get it out of his system before he saw her again – he'd been lucky this time, and he didn't want to lose control again.

NINE

"Now remember, girls, your goal tonight is to find a compatible male alien, and persuade him to join you in one of the coupling capsules at the Cantina. The future of the Colony is riding on you, girls, so drink your fertility boosters, and let's go!" Donna raised her cup, and waited for them all to follow suit. When she was satisfied, she said, "To a future with lots of babies!"

They all repeated the toast and drank the bitter tasting brew, though Dani almost brought hers back up again, she was so nervous. The dress she was wearing didn't help, either. It was a white clingy thing that showed more skin than it covered, and ended just below her bottom. Worse, it hadn't come with any underwear, so every step she took, she was terrified her dress would ride up and she'd moon everybody. Add that to the ridiculously high heels that felt like stilts and it was only a matter of time before she tripped, fell flat on her face with her bare arse in the air, and embarrassed everybody.

"Don't chew off your lipstick," Franny

chided, taking Dani's makeup kit from her nerveless hands to reapply the lip colour for her.

"What about Rue?" Dani asked, when Franny was finished. "She needs lipstick, too."

"Just a shimmer of gloss for Rue. Don't want to take the focus off those stunning eyes," Franny cooed, as she swiped some glittery gloss over Rue's lips.

When Donna was satisfied that they were all ready, she pressed her palm to the pad beside the outer door and it hissed open. "Into the skimmers, girls, quickly!"

They piled in, all laughing and chattering nervously in excitement at their first night out in the Colony. A night without Donna, it turned out, when she didn't exit any of the skimmers at their destination.

Neon lights announced that they'd arrived at the One Shot Cantina, which was shaped like an igloo made of limestone on the outside. Inside, the booths had the same limestone look, blending into the interior walls, which were decorated with what looked like weapons. Ray guns out of some old science fiction movie.

"Let's all grab a drink, and wait for the men to arrive. The Intergalactic Dating Agency has booked out the entire place for the night, so any man here is looking for love just as much as you are. So don't be shy!" Flora shouted.

Somehow, everyone else seemed to

have a drink to raise as they shouted their agreement with Flora, who appeared to be in charge tonight. Dani breathed a sigh of relief.

Dani weaved through the crowd to put her back to the (fake) stone wall, where she might see the men as they walked through the door.

"You should be up the front, with the rest of the temptresses," Rue said to her. "Once these guys get a look at you in that dress, there'll be a battle royale for you, and no one will even look at the rest of us." She huffed out a breath. "A good thing, too. If any of these desperate fuckers lay a hand on me, they'll lose it." She held up a pair of shears and snipped the air with them, before sticking them back in her pocket.

Now Dani wished she'd thought to bring a weapon – or that she'd been wearing something with somewhere to put it.

"If you want my advice, don't pick the ones undressing you with their eyes. Pick one who's nervous, whose eyes look at you with longing. Someone who knows he doesn't deserve you, but he already worships the ground you walk on."

Dani laughed. She was an orphan who'd never been anywhere or done anything, and her only skills were basic farming and not falling out of this dress…yet, at least. None of the men here deserved her – they likely deserved a lot better. Like Rue, who knew everything there was to know about farming. Or Franny, who could cook and paint and do amazing makeup. Or Flora who…

"Heads up. Here they come."

Aliens. So many of them. Big ones. Hairy ones. Ones with horns. Skin every colour of the rainbow.

And…her dentist.

Dani's eyes met his and her heart stopped.

TEN

"Excuse me, sir, but you cannot enter the event unless you sign this first." A tablet was thrust in front of Fang's face, covered in small print.

He scanned the contract, his annoyance growing with every line he read. "What's this about children? If a child results from my activities tonight, I assume full responsibility for it? I haven't even met a girl yet, and you expect in the next four hours, I'll not only meet one, but get to know her well enough she'll be carrying my child?"

"Standard contract, sir. No sign, no entry."

Claw barged in front of Fang, seized the tablet and signed his name. Then he handed it back to Fang. "Just sign it. Wear a condom, if you want. I brought three boxes." He shoved one into Fang's pocket and waited, staring pointedly at the table.

"Oh, fine, then." Fang signed his name.

"Enjoy your night, sir." The waiter or whatever he was thrust his tablet at the next man.

Talon appeared at Fang's side. "Ready to help an old bear get laid?"

Fang scanned the room. A flash of gold caught his eye, then held it, before his eyes drifted down to her face. Whoever she was, she was absolutely lovely. Golden hair piled atop a heart-shaped face, with blood-red lips that begged to be kissed. All he could see of her dress was the white collar that circled her neck, but he didn't need to see anything below the neck to know she was the most beautiful woman in the room, and the one he wanted to spend the night with.

"The old bear can fend for himself. I feel like hunting tonight," Fang said.

Talon gave a whoop, but Fang ignored him, headed to the bar. "A glass of baijiu for me, and a drink for the lady in the white dress over there." He pointed at the golden beauty. Come to think of it, her hair was the same colour as Dandelion's, though she looked older. Maybe he should have picked someone who didn't remind him of one of his patients. A busty brunette, like the one eyeing him from the other end of the bar.

But his eyes found their way back to the golden girl…only to discover she'd vanished.

"Wait, where is she?"

The bartender just shrugged and asked for payment. Absently, Fang swiped his chip across the scanner, waiting for it to beep its acceptance before he seized both glasses and set off in search of the girl.

ELEVEN

"Ladies, find your tables. In a moment, once you have all taken your seats, the gentlemen will join you," announced a shirtless little man with hooves instead of feet. "Just pick the table with your number on it and sit down."

Dani looked around desperately for the table marked with a six. It was on the far side of the room, right in front of a sign that pointed to the coupling capsules. Well, she wouldn't have to go far, if she wanted to have her way with the hot alien vampire. She would not think of him as a dentist, because he wasn't at work, and she wasn't in that awful chair, with all those whirring things on the table in front of her and…

"Hello, little virgin. I know you have orders to seduce a man tonight. I'll save you the trouble, if you just stand up right now and say you've chosen me for the night." The voice was dark and seductive, just like its owner, but she'd never seen this man before in her life. How could he possibly know she'd never…?

"I said now, little flower, and I'll pop

your cherry so quick, you won't even feel it. If you don't, I'll make your deflowering so slow and painful, you'll never want another man again. Because Falcon promised you to me tonight, and I will have you, but the longer you make me wait to fuck you, the more I'll make you hurt."

Dani's heart fluttered in her chest. Last night she thought she'd been scared, but that was nothing compared to the terror turning her insides to ice right now. Her mouth opened, but no sound came out. She couldn't even cry for help. This horrible, hateful man was going to drag her away and do hurtful things to her and she couldn't…

She'd give anything to see her dentist right now.

TWELVE

There she was, sitting at a table right at the back of the Cantina, with fear so powerful radiating off her, Fang fancied he could feel it himself. And the source of it? The shady looking incubus sitting across from her, who had her transfixed in terror. Worse, he was enjoying this, the bastard, drinking in her fear like a vampire gorging on blood.

How dare he?

Vampires were far more powerful than incubi, and he was going to make this one regret even looking her way.

First, Fang gathered up her fear, winding the chaotic strands into a hard ball in his hand, until he'd claimed it all. Next, he wrapped the ball in layers of his own anger at the incubus's audacity.

Then he heard the idiot's final words to her: "The longer you make me wait to fuck you, the more I'll make you hurt."

In Fang's fury, he crushed that ball into something as densely packed as a neutron star, if stars were invisible balls of emotion and energy and not matter.

Then, he threw it at the incubus.

The man's head jerked sideways. His

eyes rolled up into his head, before he slumped over on the table, out for the count.

Fang lifted up the chair and tipped the idiot out onto the floor, then kicked him under the table. Finally, he took the seat for his own and placed her drink in front of her. "I'm sorry for taking so long to get to you. The drink service here is terribly slow."

"Thank you," she said, her eyes shimmering with tears. "You saved me."

Fang shrugged, and sipped from his glass. "Anything else you need, just let me know."

"I want to leave, but I need…" She gulped.

He cast his mind back, remembering the things the incubus had said before he threatened her. Perhaps a night with a princess might be possible after all. "I believe I can help you with that. I have an offer for you. Unlike this idiot," he gave the incubus another kick under the table, "if you just hear me out, I might just be able to give you everything you want."

THIRTEEN

An eager YES danced on the tip of her tongue, but Dani pressed her lips together and just nodded instead.

"You are a virgin and you are here to change that, yes?"

Another nod. If she didn't, Donna would punish her for sure.

"I would be honoured if you'll allow

me to make your first time both pleasurable and memorable, if you will accept my company for the night. I can't promise I won't bite – I am a vampire, after all, and my venom has the power to take away pain and help you relax, both of which will allow you to enjoy your first time so much more than without it – but I will swear to you that I will not hurt you, and instead will do my best between now and dawn to worship you as fervently as any goddess."

Oh GOD. If she'd been wearing underwear, they'd have melted about halfway through that little speech. As it was, she clenched her thighs together, trying to hide the blooming heat in her core.

What had Donna said she had to do,

in order to secure a room and some privacy to seduce the man she wanted? Oh, that's right.

Dani shot to her feet. "I've made my choice." She pointed a shaking finger at the vampire who'd saved her, whose offer she could not refuse.

FOURTEEN

The room fell silent as the bar manager made his way over to them. "The first match has been made, and the best room in the house goes to…" He raised his eyebrows.

"Dani," the girl whispered.

"Dani, and…" He turned to Fang, his eyes widening in shock. "You're not

Shade!"

Fang turned on the full force of his smile for the barman. "No, I'm Dr Fang."

The barman's fear tasted bitter, but he managed a smile and said, "Dani and Dr Fang! Everyone give them a round of applause to wish them a good night, while I take them to our finest room!"

Fang offered her his arm, and together they followed the man to a door marked SHACKLED TOGETHER HONEYMOON SUITE. The man turned the key in the lock, then threw the door open wide. "Enjoy," he said.

Dani stepped inside first, with Fang close behind her. Not a moment too soon, for the barman slammed the door shut the moment he was through it.

"Oh my God," she whispered.

Fang didn't believe in deities, but he did believe he'd never seen so many handcuffs and shackles in one place in his life. Shackled together, indeed.

At least there was a bed, with plenty of pillows. She could lie there in comfort while he took care of her every need.

But…first things first. "Can I kiss you?" he asked.

FIFTEEN

Before she'd finished saying yes, his lips were on hers. Just like she'd dreamed last night, cool and firm and commanding, so she couldn't help but open her mouth for more. And it was almost like he could read her mind, because he gave her exactly what she wanted.

Her tongue danced with his, and he

tasted almost like citrus. No, like champagne, with a fizz that infused deep into her blood. Just like when he'd bitten her and it had felt like…

He broke the kiss and ducked his head, wiping his mouth on the back of his hand. "Please forgive me. I don't know what's gotten into me. My venom sacs don't normally do that, and definitely not on a first date. Perhaps I should kiss you somewhere else instead until I can get them under control."

He dropped his lips to her neck.

Dani felt lightheaded. Perhaps it was the venom she'd inadvertently swallowed. "This won't…poison me, will it?" she asked. "Or turn me into a vampire, too?"

He chuckled. "Oh, of course not. My

venom only relaxes you and dulls pain. Turning you into a vampire would require us drinking a large quantity of each other's blood, which would leave us quite lethargic, and me unable to give you the memorable night of first-time sex that I promised. As it is, it might be some time before I can bite you, as my venom sacs appear to be empty, something that's never happened before. But there's plenty more of you I can taste, while I recover."

Vampires suffered from premature ejaculation of their venom sacs, Dani realised slowly. There was so much she didn't know about aliens, or even just vampires.

"You wish for me to stop?"

Dani realised she was still shaking her

head. She stopped. "No, I don't want you to stop. I want…more kisses. Please."

"As you wish."

His mouth descended on her neck once more, before he kissed his way down to her collar. He continued down the V between her breasts, and the champagne trail in her blood followed him, all the way down to her navel before it settled in her core.

His hands slid up her thighs, catching the hem of her dress as he edged that upward, too, until he gasped. "You're not wearing any underwear." He dropped to his knees, where he couldn't help but see all of her private parts, on full display.

She wanted to squirm away from his

scrutiny, until she felt his lips on her thigh, freezing her in place.

"Open your legs a little more, so that I can taste you," he said.

His breath wafted inside her, and she couldn't move. Couldn't think.

Strong hands parted her, then his tongue rasped over her flesh, lingering on her clit until she feared her knees would no longer hold her. She was going to melt into a puddle on the floor in three…two…

Two firm hands cupped her bottom, lifting her legs over his shoulders. "Wrap your legs around me," he said, and she did, hanging on for dear life as he devoured her.

The noises coming out of her mouth were more animal than human, but she couldn't seem to stop. Didn't want to stop as his tongue spiralled her pleasure higher and higher, his hands kneading her arse like she needed.

"Oh my God, FANG!" she cried out as what had to be an actual orgasm exploded in her core, bigger and better than anything she'd imagined in her dreams.

She was dimly aware of him carrying her to the bed, as soft sheets replaced his hands beneath her bottom so he could wrench the barely there dress off her completely. Until she lay naked on the bed before him, staring up at a body that belonged to a statue more than a man. Every muscle clearly defined beneath his skin, from the strong arms that had lifted her effortlessly, to the ridged abs she wanted to lick, and down to…

"Will you be able to fit that inside me?" she blurted out.

The statue moved and smiled. "When you're ready for me, I will give you all of this, and you'll want more," he said.

She licked her lips. That sounded amazing. Better than a dream. "Do it. Give it to me."

"But I have more pleasure to give you first, before you are ready for me. Be patient, my princess." He climbed onto the bed, and stalked toward her. He pressed his lips to her thigh. "So sweet. Would you let me bite you, right here?"

"Yes." It came out as a moan of longing.

But he didn't bite her. Instead, he slid his finger inside her, thrusting slowly in and out as if he was testing her, before giving her all of him. "So incredibly tight. Once I'm inside you, I'll never want to leave, Dani."

Her heart skipped a beat as his tongue caressed her name.

Then he added a second finger to the first, stretching her, and she gasped.

"See? Not ready for me yet. But you will be. I promised you a night of pleasure, and it will be all pleasure."

Oh God, yes. She couldn't move. Couldn't think about anything but his fingers, sliding in and out of her, as he touched his tongue to her clit.

His tongue spiralled more slowly this time, matching the steady thrust of his fingers, pushing just a little bit deeper each time as he pulled her closer and closer to the edge of another climax.

"Please, oh, please," she heard herself say.

Instead of relenting, he took his tongue away, only to replace it a moment later with the rough pad of his thumb. Closer…closer…oh, so close…

Something sharp stung her thigh, flooding her veins with champagne bubbles a moment before her orgasm hit, and she could neither see nor hear, only feel as pleasure flowed through her, wave after wave after wave.

"Good girl." His growl dragged her vision back to his face, as she felt a third finger slide inside her, stretching her even more. "You're so wet. Almost ready for me. But I need you to come for me again, Dani. Will you come for me?"

Anything, she tried to say, but all that came out was a wordless moan as his fingers rubbed against a sensitive spot inside her, perfectly in time with the press of his thumb on her clit. Maybe he was moving his fingers faster this time, or maybe she just wanted it more, but this next orgasm came rushing toward her without warning, and she wanted…

"Come for me, Dani," he growled.

"Only…if…you bite me…" she panted, even as she felt her control slipping.

She barely registered the scrape of his fangs on her other thigh before twin waves of euphoria crashed into her, multiplying her pleasure a thousandfold as his venom combined with her orgasm. It felt so incredible she feared she'd cry.

When her vision cleared, she found herself sitting on Fang's lap, wrapped in his arms. "How do you feel?" he asked.

She looked up into his eyes, his gaze so tender she couldn't stop the tears now. "Wonderful," she wept. And yet…"I want more."

"I'll give you more, if you want it. I'll give you everything. Are you ready for me, Dani?" He took her hand and wrapped it around his cock, the hard length of him trapped between his body and hers. When she nodded, he said, "Then put your hands on my shoulders and rise up onto your knees, straddling my lap."

She tried to do as he asked, but her legs were shaky, so he wrapped an arm around her waist to steady her, while his other hand held his cock in readiness for her.

"Just sink down slowly, taking as much as you want," he said.

The head of his cock touched her clit, and she was surprised at how hot it felt, compared to the coolness of the rest of his body. Then that glorious heat was inside her, that endless length sliding upward until he filled her completely. She expected pain, but there was nothing but pleasure and heat and him. And then he began to move, holding tight to her waist as he thrust with agonising slowness, almost like he was afraid to hurt her, when every stroke sent bubbles of pleasure straight from her clit deep into her core.

"Such a good girl," he growled, before

he fastened his mouth over her nipple and sucked hard.

She threw her head back and screamed as her core detonated. Once. Twice. That wasn't possible, was it? She didn't care if it was impossible. She wanted… "More," Dani gasped.

SIXTEEN

Fang truly didn't know what was wrong with him. When he'd kissed her, his venom sacs had exploded into her mouth, without his fangs even breaking the skin. When she'd come on his tongue, she'd tasted like ambrosia, and he still must have been drunk on her essence when he'd begged to bite her, even though she'd already drunk all of his venom, only to empty his venom sacs into her thigh. Those few drops of blood he'd swallowed drove him into a mad frenzy, for he was certain he must have hurt her. Why else would she beg him to bite her again?

Then he'd held her shuddering body for what felt like an eternity until the venom had healed her enough to speak so she could tell him what he'd done wrong.

But then she'd wrapped her hand around his cock and asked for more…It had taken every shred of his self-control not to thrust up, deep inside her, as she'd bravely lowered herself onto his lap. He'd waited every moment for a hiss of pain or a wince from her, but it appeared all that venom had done its work well, freeing her from pain so she only felt pleasure.

Whereas Dani's flesh wrapped so tightly around his cock wasn't just pleasurable, it was absolutely exquisite. Just as he'd suspected, he wanted to stay inside her forever. Then she began to move exactly right, and it was all he could do not to explode early.

So he focussed on her pleasure instead, listening for that little hitch in her breathing that meant she was close, but then he'd gotten distracted by her delicious breasts, bobbing so beautifully before his face, and he hardly knew what he was doing before he took one nipple in his teeth and…

Stars, when she squeezed his cock like

that, he'd almost lost his mind.

Still she begged for more.

He wasn't going to be able to resist her much longer, he knew. Next time she clenched down on his cock, he'd blow right along with her.

He tipped her onto her back, into a pile of pillows, her hair spreading out beneath her like a golden halo. So beautiful.

He lifted her legs up over his shoulders, leaning in to give her more of him, just like she wanted, thrusting to the hilt, hoping he wouldn't hurt her.

"More, please," she begged.

Stars, he wasn't going to last much longer. And, black holes take him for a selfish bastard, but he wanted to hear her screaming when he came.

He'd gotten the angle just right, her breathy little moans told him, and he pounded into her, desperate to push her to the brink before he finished.

"Come for me, Dani," he growled, before the world went white.

When his vision cleared, he had his lips against her throat, and the taste of her blood on his tongue. His cock was still wedged into her heavenly heat, but it wouldn't be long before he slipped out, and he needed to clean up the mess he'd made. Actually, he should probably make a start on that while she was still lying there, stunned.

Stars, he hoped he hadn't taken too much blood. He'd never lost control like that before. If he'd hurt her…

He washed up at a small basin in the

corner of the room, then brought a towel over to take care of her, too. Just looking at her wet pussy had him hardening for another round. He'd promised her a whole night of pleasure, and he intended to keep his word.

She blinked at him, then smiled.

His heart swelled in his chest. "How do you feel?" he enquired, as if they were in his clinic, instead of in a kink bordello where he'd just fucked her within an inch of her life.

Her eyes lit up. "I've never felt more loved in my life." Then joy turned to horror. "Oh my God, I have to go!" She leaped off the bed, struggled into her dress, and was halfway out the door before he had the presence of mind to call after her.

"When can I see you again?"

"Next speed dating thing, maybe?" But it wasn't Dani's voice – instead, the officious faun with the tablet stood in the doorway, not seeming to care that Fang was naked. "Now, I have a survey for you to fill out about the service you received tonight. Did it meet with your expectations?"

He hadn't had any expectations about his night here. Only to discover that meeting Dani had exceeded his wildest dreams.

And the most incredible woman he'd ever met, the first girl he'd ever even considered forever with, was gone.

Well, fuck.

SEVENTEEN

The morning after the most memorable night of her life, Dani was surprised to see the world hadn't changed. Protein bars for breakfast, washed down with vitamin water, before trudging up to the freshly turned soil in Orchard Three to plant the newly arrived orange tree seedlings. When her thighs burned every time she leaned down, or her insides ached with emptiness for the feel of Fang and his heart-stopping orgasms, she pressed her lips together and tried to ignore it.

Maybe the others hadn't enjoyed their night as much as she had. She'd left to be alone with Fang so early in the night, she hadn't even noticed which men the others had chosen to spend the night with. Ugh, maybe the arsehole Fang had saved her from had woken up and turned his horrible attentions on someone else.

Dani scanned the field, looking for signs that someone might be injured. Franny was walking a bit stiffly, but no more than she was herself. Oh, not Franny. After all the work she'd done to make everyone look good last night, the last thing she deserved was to be abused by that bastard. She tried to get a chance to speak to her over the course of the day, but Franny seemed to want to avoid everyone. Finally, after dinner, she saw Franny veer off toward the dormitories. The perfect place for a private chat, Dani told herself as she turned to follow.

"Dani, Donna wants to see you," Flora said. "She said it's urgent."

Swearing under her breath, she forced herself to follow Flora instead.

"Stars, what kept you? Quick, you need to get into the skimmer and go to the dentist. You have an appointment tonight, and you can't be late."

She got to see Dr Fang again? Dani brightened, until she realised Donna hadn't used his name. She'd called him the dentist.

Not the clinic again.

EIGHTEEN

After a dozen patients, Fang had his answer. Blood had never gotten him high before, and it had never had the effect on him that it had last night. Nor did it get him high now, on the dozen regular patients he'd offered pain relief to in his normal, professional way. So for him to experience the same phenomenon from two different women, two nights in a row, and no one else…made absolutely no sense.

One last patient, and he could do some research into things that made a vampire euphoric. It might have been something she'd consumed that lingered in her blood which had that effect on him, and not the blood itself. Or…

He glanced at his tablet. "Dandelion," he read.

His eyes met hers. Recognition flared. His cock rose to salute her.

Dandelion. Dani. Stars above, it wasn't two women, it was one, and worse, he'd slept with a patient.

Then she looked away, and wouldn't meet his eyes.

He must have hurt her last night,

when he lost control. Blithering black holes, he was an idiot.

"How do you feel? Is there any pain?" he asked.

She nodded. "A little," she said, still not looking at him.

"Let me give you something for that," he said, stepping in close behind her. He allowed himself to inhale her scent for only a moment before he bent his head to bite her neck, swallowing back his moan as a few drops of her blood hit his tongue.

"Thank you." The words sounded forced.

He'd definitely hurt her. Stars…

"If you'll just take a seat in the chair, I can check to see how well you're healing," Fang said.

She climbed stiffly into the chair, then gripped the arms with white-knuckled fingers. Still not looking at him.

"If you could just open your mouth…"

She was healing well. Not surprising, after she'd swallowed a mouthful of his venom. For all the unprofessional things he'd done – from kissing her through to giving her orgasm after screaming orgasm – at least he'd done his actual job properly, and not hurt her doing that. It was a small mercy, especially knowing he had hurt her last night…

He wanted to ask her what he'd done, and what he could possibly do to make it up to her. Stars take it, he wanted to ask her if she'd be willing to switch dentists to one of his colleagues, and go on another date with him. But he could feel the fear radiating off her, so he knew he had to wait for her to say something first, or he'd ruin any chance he had of another amazing night with her.

"Is the prescription I gave you for pain relief effective? I can give you more, if you like," he ventured.

She shook her head, then considered. "Perhaps a little more venom might help."

If he'd caused her pain, then he owed her every drop in his venom sacs. He bit her neck, trying to pump as much venom into her bloodstream as possible while taking the smallest sip of her blood. When he withdrew, he realised he still had one full venom sac. Quickly, he bit her again, giving her all he had.

Only this time, he'd struck a vein, and ended up with a mouthful of her blood that he didn't dare swallow until she was gone.

"There we go. You're all done," he mumbled with his mouth full. He managed to keep it together until she left the clinic before he bolted for the bathroom.

He dropped his pants, fisted his aching cock, took a deep breath, and swallowed.

Several minutes later, when his vision finally returned, he reached for some paper towel with a shaking hand so he could clean up.

He scanned the bathroom, confused, until…stars. Now he had to clean the ceiling. What a mess.

NINETEEN

The moment her eyes met his, she remembered what she'd said to him — that he'd made her feel loved. She'd regretted it almost the instant the words had left her lips, because no matter how wonderful the night had been, that's all he'd offered her — one night. And she'd gone and fallen for him…

So she wasn't sure what tied her belly in knots more tonight – a visit to the dentist, or her warring desire to jump on him and ride his cock for the rest of the night, or to run and hide in mortification. At least she was wearing underwear tonight, so he couldn't see how wet he made her.

But if he wanted to see her again, it was up to him to say so. She'd blundered her way into a declaration of love last night, so she'd made her interest clear. A hot vampire who could give a girl a hundred orgasms in a night likely had dozens of offers for his company. She was lucky he'd even looked at her at all.

"Is there any pain?"

It was almost like he knew how much she ached for him, but his businesslike, clinical tone made it clear he did not share her desire. He bit her so quickly she barely felt it before it was over.

He'd checked her teeth, which were healing exactly as well as he'd said they would, before he offered her more pain relief.

She wanted to beg for the kind of relief he'd given her last night, but she knew she'd only look silly. But she wasn't above asking for some more venom.

She almost wept when she felt his lips on her neck. One bite, just as quick as the first, before he swore and bit her again, lingering like he was considering giving her more. Like the kind of relief she really wanted, instead of just a taste.

For a moment, Dani dared to hope.

Then he withdrew, rushing her out of the clinic so fast she was outside before she realised what was happening, and the doors were already closing behind him as he dashed off. To spit her blood out, most likely, because he didn't want any part of her any more.

Alone in the skimmer, she let the tears fall, where no one would see, so that by the time she reached Star Farm, no one would ever know how silly she'd been.

TWENTY

The weeks came and went. There were other speed dating nights, but Donna sent other girls instead of Dani, who just went to bed, like any other night. Not that she cared. She had no desire to watch Fang bestow his glowing smile on some other lucky girl, who'd be left with one glorious night to remember for a lifetime of longing. Nor did she want to feign interest in some other man, no matter how hot an alien he was.

When she woke up one morning with her breasts aching, she welcomed it, because that meant it was her period and no one would question her if she lay in bed a little later, complaining of cramps. That evening, she lined up for her weekly health scan, wishing she could just skip it and go to bed early because she was tired. But she couldn't miss her health scan, because she needed to ask Donna for her monthly supply of pads.

Finally, it was her turn. Donna held the scanner over her belly for longer than usual. Perhaps she could actually detect that her period was about to start. "Good," Donna said, then waved for her to go. "Next!"

"Wait! My period's starting today. I need supplies," Dani said.

"No, you don't," Donna said, beckoning the next girl. "Next!"

"But – " Dani began.

"Stop wasting my time, or I'll stick you in solitary," Donna said. "Next!"

At least her period hadn't actually started yet. Maybe Dani had gotten the dates wrong, and her breasts were aching for some other reason. Aching to be cupped in a pair of long fingered hands as he lowered his lips to suck on one nipple, then the other, fangs scraping over sensitive flesh…

She'd dreamed about him last night, doing all sorts of things. It was the aftermath from the dream, that was all, that her body thought was real.

When her period didn't appear that day or the next, she breathed a sigh of relief and silently thanked Donna's no-nonsense dismissal of her mistake.

Until two days later, when Donna summoned her to her office.

She had a sofa and two straight backed chairs in there, and Dani knew better than to take the sofa. Good posture was a key element of good health, she'd heard Donna say often enough, as she straightened her back to sit properly in the plastic chair.

Then Donna left the office, only to return a moment later with the arsehole who'd threatened her at the Cantina.

"I'm sure you remember Shade, Dandelion. After all, you're carrying his child. That means, in accordance with the contract you signed with the Intergalactic Dating Agency, that you will pay for your child. Antenatal care, the birth, as well as the child's upkeep until they reach adulthood. So, if you will refer to the detailed cost outline I sent you, you can choose between a lump sum or a payment plan. Alternatively, if you wish to raise the child yourself at your own expense, our only payment option is a lump sum, as once you take sole custody of the child, we waive all responsibility for it. So, which option do you prefer?"

Dani couldn't seem to close her mouth. Pregnant? To this guy? No, there had to be a mistake.

"I didn't fuck the bitch, even if you

and Falcon promised her to me. Some other guy's the father, not me, even though I paid for her. And you're not going to get another cent out of me unless you rip the baby out of this slut's womb, and then personally hold her down while I fuck her until she's carrying my kid, like I paid for." Shade leaned over Donna, like he meant to hit her or something.

"He's right, Donna, we never –" Dani began, only to be cut off by an explosion of pain in her cheek.

"Shut up, slut, unless you want me to slap you again," Shade warned.

Dani tasted blood and wisely decided to stay silent. She wished she could leave, but she knew she couldn't unless Donna dismissed her. And she didn't want to leave Donna alone with this horrible violent man, either.

Donna rose jerkily from her seat, her face unusually pale. "So sorry, Mr Shade. I won't take any more of your valuable time, and I shall notify you when the procedure is complete."

A moment later, she was ushering Shade out of her office.

Dani only had a moment alone, but her thoughts whirled faster than she could follow. She was pregnant? With Fang's child? How wonderful. Maybe she would get to see him again, after all, especially if they had a child together.

When Donna returned, her face had gone from white to red with anger. "Whose child are you carrying?" she shouted.

Dani shrank away from the enraged woman. "Fang. Doctor Fang. The alien vampire I met at the speed dating event at the Cantina. He took me to bed and he…" Oh God, she couldn't tell Donna all the things he'd done to her. All the wonderful, wonderful things, culminating in this, the most wonderful of all. Dani swallowed. "He's the father of my child."

"A doctor, eh?"

Dani didn't bother to correct her. She had her tablet out, and was already searching for him.

"Ohhh, interesting. Very interesting. Perhaps we can salvage something out of this situation, even if you were stupid enough to open your legs for the wrong man. But a bidding war between two rich men might make it all worth it. You might even get to keep the child."

Wait…what? They'd take her baby away from her? They couldn't. Even back on Earth they wouldn't separate a mother from her child without good reason. Then it dawned on her – Donna had promised Shade she'd have a procedure.

"I won't have an abortion. I won't! You can't make me!" Dani cried, cradling her belly even though she couldn't feel the child inside her. She knew it was there. The baby she and Fang had made.

"Shut up and go away, you stupid girl. You'll do whatever I tell you to. Well, unless Shade takes you, and you'll be his problem then." Donna ignored her and turned to her tablet to furiously take notes.

Dani swallowed. She wanted to defend herself, to defend the child she was carrying, but it was a miracle Donna hadn't already sent her to solitary. Perhaps she should just take her good luck where she could find it, and leave before anything worse happened.

And find a way to get word to Fang about the baby. He wouldn't let Shade and Donna kill it, she was certain.

TWENTY-ONE

Dani hadn't been at any of the other speed dating nights, and now she'd missed an appointment. A sensible man would leave her alone, as she obviously wanted to avoid him, but he just couldn't stop thinking about her. Maybe he'd misread things. Maybe…maybe…

Maybe he should try to contact her

and ask her what he'd done wrong. If she didn't want to see or talk to him, she could say so, and he'd leave her alone for good.

The only thing was…she didn't seem to exist on any of the Colony databases. The only contact details for her were Star Farm, but when he called, her bulldog of a secretary answered, saying she was unavailable, so he hung up again.

Finally, he made up his mind. The only way to find her was to sneak into Star Farm so he could see her, face to face.

Entering Star Farm was easy. The wall of administration buildings at the entrance were all dark, so he skirted them and headed deeper into the place. Fresh turned soil and more plants than he'd seen since leaving Tito assaulted his nostrils as he headed away from the empty buildings to the ones where people were.

The most populated building was also dark, but the slow and steady heartbeats of the people inside told him it was a dormitory of some kind. Sure enough, that's what it was — one big barn of a place, with beds lined up like a military camp. Half the beds were empty, likely because a bunch of the girls were at tonight's speed dating event, but he knew Dani wasn't there, which meant she had to be here somewhere.

His breath caught in his throat as he spotted a blonde braid stretched out across a pillow, only to see that the girl wasn't her.

A princess like Dani wouldn't bed

down here among the farm girls, surely, Fang told himself, when the third blonde girl also proved to not be his quarry. He'd almost made his way to the other end of the dormitory without finding her, when one girl turned from one side to the other, throwing her blankets off for a moment before snuggling under them again. In that moment, Fang saw a telltale flash of gold, and he ran to see.

It was her!

But they couldn't speak here. If any of the girls woke up and saw him, he'd never hear the end of it. Prometheus would probably make him tomorrow's headline news story – Vampire Stalker Caught by Plucky Young Farm Girls or some such drivel.

He scooped Dani up in his arms and fled the scene.

TWENTY-TWO

God, it was cold in the dormitory tonight. Had she kicked off her blankets in her sleep again? As Dani blinked the sleep from her eyes, feeling around for the lost blankets, she froze. There were no blankets or sheets. Just cold vinyl and steel, like she was in a dentist's clinic.

She couldn't help it. She screamed.

"Please, don't. It's just me, and I'd never hurt you." The whisper came from across the room, before he turned on the light.

Dani almost cried, she was so happy to see Fang. "How did I get here?"

He ducked his head. "I sneaked into the farm, and brought you here."

"You kidnapped me? Is it because of the baby? You'll help me save it, right?" she asked eagerly.

"What baby?"

He didn't know? The story spilled out of her, from finding out she was pregnant right down to Shade. "And if you don't help me, Donna and Shade are going to force me to have an abortion, and kill our baby."

He looked stunned. "I don't know

what to say, but I promise I'll do everything I can to help you."

"Thank you!" She threw her arms around his neck and kissed him. Then she pulled away. "So why did you bring me here?"

"I…you missed an appointment, and I was worried. Then when you didn't turn up at the Cantina again, I called Star Farm, and when they wouldn't let me talk to you…I need to know what I did that night. Why you don't want to see me," he said.

"Of course I want to see you. That night was wonderful, more wonderful than I could have possibly imagined, but you did only offer me one night, and I thought…" she began, feeling blood rush to her face.

"But why are you so afraid of me? I can feel your fear, and I can see how tightly your hands are clenched around the arms of my chair. What did I do to scare you so much? Please tell me. I'll do anything to make it up to you." He really did sound desperate.

Dani wet her lips. It was so embarrassing, but she couldn't let him go on believing a lie. "I'm not scared of you. You're probably the person I trust most in the entire Altan System, if not the whole galaxy. But the one thing in the universe that scares me is dentists."

His eyes darkened with fury. "Tell me the name of the dentist who hurt you."

If only it were that easy. "He didn't hurt me, but…he made grown men scream." Dani sighed. "All right. His name was P Sherman, 42 Wallaby Way, Sydney." At Fang's blank look, she added, "The dentist from the old Disney cartoon, *Finding Nemo*? They used to play it constantly at the orphanage where I grew up, to show us what the Great Barrier Reef looked like before most of it got bleached to death. Anyway, there's this dentist…the whole story is about the fish in the tank in his clinic, which he steals from the reef when he goes diving. But in the background, he has a steady stream of patients, and they're all in terrible pain, screaming, while the fish watch, until they find a way to escape." She screwed up her face. "I know it doesn't make any sense, but that's the thing about an irrational fear of dentists. It's irrational."

Fang began to laugh. "That's it? You're afraid of dentists because of a film you watched as a child?"

"Tell me none of your clients have screamed in your clinic," she challenged him.

"Not a single one. One bite and they relax. There's a reason I'm the best dentist in the Colony," Fang said.

"None of your patients have ever screamed?" Surely there had to be one.

Suddenly he was right there beside her. "I made you scream. But not here. In the bed at the Cantina. I could make you scream again here, if you like."

God, would she ever. Only…not here. Anywhere but here. "If you took me back to your place, or at least somewhere there's a bed…"

Fang slowly shook his head. "Do you know how to cure an irrational fear? It is possible, if you're willing to try. The first step is to face your fears, in a way where you feel safe and in control." He pulled on the lab coat he usually wore when he was working. "Do you trust me, Dani?"

"Yes. Yes, I trust you. But this place…" She waved her hands at the chair, the instruments. "I don't want to be here." She stood up and moved toward the door. To her surprise, he didn't even try to stop her.

"Dani…what if you were in control, and not the dentist?"

Then someone was definitely going to get hurt. "I wouldn't know what I was doing. I could do something wrong with one of those things."

"Turn around and look at me, Dani. What would you like to do to me right now?"

Not hurt him. She definitely didn't want to hurt him. And he was being so kind, so she really owed him an answer, but… Dani took a deep breath and forced herself to turn around. "Holy FUCK."

Wearing nothing but his dentist's coat, Fang stretched out in the chair, beckoning to her. She let her eyes drift lower. His cock was pointing right at her, like it was trying to say I WANT YOU. All those muscles, glistening blue in the light of the cabinets, reminding her just how alien he was, but she didn't care. She wanted to climb on top of him and lick them all, up and down and right back up again.

"I know what I want. I want you to take all your clothes off, then come up here and sit on my face," Fang said.

YES! A voice in the back of her mind screamed, as she reached for the hem of her nightgown.

But he was lying on a dentist's chair. Wearing that white coat.

"Do you want to feel my tongue inside you again, Dani? Do you want me to bite you, just before I make you scream?"

Yes. She'd give anything to feel like that again. Her nightgown drifted to the floor, forgotten, as she kicked off her knickers. She took a step toward him, then another.

But he was on the chair…

Strong hands seized her around the

waist, lifting her until she straddled his chest, with her legs hanging off either side of the chair.

"Get on your knees, and sit on my face," he coaxed, his hands holding her steady.

Dani took another deep breath, and obeyed.

"Ohhh, good girl," he said. A slight sting as he bit her inner thigh, but before she could even gasp in surprise, he thrust his tongue inside her.

"Oh my God," she cried, reaching blindly for something, anything, to hold onto while Fang devoured her.

It seemed only a moment before the first orgasm ripped through her, quickly followed by the second. Another sting on her other thigh, before she screamed all the way through the third.

He rubbed his chin against her clit, rough stubble driving her wild.

"There's my good girl. What do you want me to do to you next?"

Her mind was blank. "I want more."

"And I'll give you more. Now slide down my body, until you can feel exactly what I want to give you."

His hands guided her hips as she slowly slid down him, shuffling backward on her knees until she could feel the hot, hard length of him between her thighs.

Just like that first night, he lifted her so that she was right above him, then took his cock in his spare hand to position it at exactly the right angle.

"Take what you want from me, Dani.

I'm so ready for you."

She'd forgotten just how big he was. She eased down slowly, gripping the arms of the chair to help her push herself down, moaning as he stretched her so deliciously she could think of nothing else but his cock and how much she wanted him.

"Good girl. Any time you need filling, my cock is ready and waiting for you. You'll come when you need me, right, Dani?"

He felt so good inside her. She didn't want to move, she was so full.

"Now ride me, Dani. Take all the pleasure you want from me. I'm all yours."

Tentatively, she rocked her hips. Forward, then back, grinding against him.

"Harder, Dani. Faster."

"I can't. You're so big. Help me."

His hands fastened around her hips again, moving her body effortlessly against his. Harder and faster and…

"Oh God, Fang, I'm coming!"

"Good girl. Now come for me again."

She rode him for what felt like hours, losing count of how many orgasms he'd given her, until suddenly he slowed.

"Dani, I can't hold on much longer. I'm close to coming for you, just for you. Would you like me to bite you?"

"Yes, oh, please."

He reared up, driving his cock deeper inside her than she'd thought possible, then fastened his lips around her nipple. A sharp sting…

"Dani! Stars, I love you, Dani!" he roared, pouring himself into her. Wave after wave, sweeping her away until all she could do was cling to him as she screamed his name.

TWENTY-THREE

No one noticed Dani slip back into the dormitory just before dawn, or how she winced as she climbed into bed.

No one heard her silent promise to the baby within her that Fang would take care of them. He loved her. He'd promised.

And no one saw the tears she shed

when she realised all this seemed too good to be true, which was why the universe might take it all away again, because she didn't deserve Fang or this much happiness or any of this.

TWENTY-FOUR

After Dani left, and he was done cleaning up the mess they'd made in the clinic, Fang finally sat down to do some research. He'd found no reference to any substance that could induce euphoria in a vampire, legal or otherwise. As for a vampire conceiving a child, well, he knew it was possible, because his parents had had him, but they'd been properly mated for a decade before he came along. He didn't even know the first thing about a vampire mating ceremony, because he'd never expected to have one. The few vampires in the Colony were mostly male, and he preferred women. Well, one woman, whose blood was like a drug to him, even before she was carrying his child. Which shouldn't be possible, but…

Fang sighed, and sent a message to the Coven Leader, one of the few female vampires in the Colony. A crone who'd entered her second century, if he remembered rightly.

He expected to have to make an appointment, but she sent a message right back, telling him to come over and visit. Elsewhere in the Colony, dawn was breaking, but in the residential levels of the Nyx Dome, the sun never rose. They lived in eternal night, because all the residents of Nyx were creatures of the night, of one kind or another.

And Coven Leader Lavinia was a more powerful creature than most, even in the Colony. There were stories that she had dragon ancestry, a fact she'd never denied.

Looking at her, Fang believed it.

"Ah, young Fang. What brings you here? Are you asking me to pass judgement?"

Fang shook his head. "No, Coven Leader. I'm not in dispute with anyone at the moment."

"Then what is so urgent that you

would visit me so close to dawn?"

Then she kept to the old ways, sleeping through the day and living through the night, even though Nyx allowed them to keep whatever hours they pleased.

"I wish to ask about mating ceremonies," he said.

"You have found a mate? Unusual for the male to come to me first. Usually it is the female, eager to find out how to secure her mate, especially if she wants children." Lavinia's bright eyes regarded him over her teacup as she sipped something that definitely wasn't tea.

"It's…yes, in part it's about children, and mating…and…how do vampires mate, exactly?"

"Surely you don't need me to explain

how to have sex, young Fang. There are plenty of films and manuals available on your tablet. With detailed pictures and everything."

She was growing impatient. He was running out of time.

"I've gotten a human girl pregnant. I drank some of her blood – just the tiniest bit – and it was like a drug, the most incredible high, and we had sex…"

"Usually required for a pregnancy to occur, as you would know if you consulted those films and manuals, young Fang." Now she was laughing at him.

"Yes, but…I thought it was rare, and you needed two vampires, and I don't understand how her blood can have that effect on me. No one else's, just hers."

Lavinia grinned and lifted her teacup in a toast. "Then congratulations, Fang, for I believe you have found your mate! A mating ceremony isn't necessary, of course, especially as it seems you've likely already fulfilled the requirements, or there wouldn't be a child. There is a child, isn't there?"

"Well, Dani said there was, but it's very early in the pregnancy, so she isn't showing yet. But I can't imagine she'd lie about a baby. Not when she's so worried about it." Come to think of it, he should have asked more about the baby. Whether it was his, and whether he could see the test results. Just to make sure. He'd go back to Star Farm and ask her tonight.

Lavinia nodded. "Well, a mating

ceremony is all about threes. Three bites a day, over three days, and sex at least once during the three days, though some couples do it all three days, just to be sure, and who can blame them? In an official ceremony, with guests and witnesses, those first three bites are public, and witnessed. The second day is usually decreed a honeymoon day, or night, for the consummation, and on the morning of the third day, just before dawn, they do the three final bites to seal the mating. For a child, as opposed to an official mating, it's only really the first three bites you need, and you're mated enough to be fertile. It doesn't matter who bites who, as long as you're both willing. Consent is even more important to a vampire, as I'm sure you know."

"Yes, Coven Leader. I have the consent of all my patients in writing before I bite them. Dani…sometimes she consents, and sometimes she's the one asking me to bite her." He considered adding that sometimes she asked when they weren't having sex, but he wasn't sure he wanted to discuss that with his Coven Leader. Or anyone except Dani.

"Well, if she wants a vampire mating ceremony, I will be happy to officiate, though we don't get many Humans who want that. Usually they want a marriage, with a wedding. All kissing and cake, while the important stuff happens afterwards." She chuckled. "Or before, if the couple do things arse-about, like you and your young lady."

"And her blood making me high? How does that fit into it?" Fang asked.

"It's fate's way of making you pay attention, boy. Not everyone gets a fated mate, so if you do, fate wants to make sure you can't just walk away. No, you're addicted to her very life essence. Very hard to ignore."

"I don't intend to ignore her. I intend to make her mine in every way possible." If she was truly his mate, he wouldn't rest until she was his. No way was he losing his family to some shady incubus she met at the pub.

TWENTY-FIVE

"How do you know the child is even mine?"

"DNA analysis is quite conclusive. Testing indicates that the child is yours."

Fang liked Dani's secretary even less in person, he decided. Then again, she was asking him for money so that she might separate him from his and Dani's child.

"Enough. I want to talk to Dani," he said.

"Dandelion is not currently available." She delivered the line so smoothly, she must have done it a thousand times before.

But she evidently hadn't used it to try and separate a vampire from his mate.

"You keep saying that. What I want to know is…when will she be available? She's already missed a dental appointment, against my advice, and she will of course need proper antenatal care throughout the pregnancy, to ensure both she and the baby are healthy. As the father of her child, I insist on being present at those appointments."

Donna rolled her eyes. "You can insist all you like. The mother's rights take precedence over whatever you want, and Dandelion does not wish to see you until you have demonstrated that you will financially support this child, as you have already stated in writing that you will do. If you will only choose a payment plan, I can make the relevant medical reports available to you. Of course, you understand that you will be liable for the cost of her antenatal care…"

"Stardust!" Fang exploded. "Free healthcare, and antenatal services in particular, are the right of every Colony citizen. Dani will receive the best of care available in the Altan System, no matter who the father of her child is!"

He almost admired the ease with which the woman changed track. Like back on Earth, she'd been a skilled saleswoman. "Ah, but she is carrying a Human-Titan hybrid, which will require specialist care every step of the way. The child might not be viable, in which case…"

"And I suppose you expect me to pay for an abortion, too?" Fang demanded.

"If you no longer want the child, and wish the pregnancy to be terminated, then the same terms apply, as though you accepted responsibility for the child yourself at birth. We will only accept a lump sum payment, not a payment plan, as the only ongoing cost will be the mother's health before, during and after the procedure."

This woman knew nothing about vampires. Children were so rare among his kind, no one would dare terminate a vampire baby. It just wasn't done. "You're not killing my baby!" he growled.

"Very well. Then you have a decision to make. Either we care for the child within our community, and you pay for its upkeep, or you claim it at birth. Which will it be?"

"What about Dani? What happens to the child's mother?"

"Dandelion will carry the child to term, after which the child will either be surrendered to you, cared for as part of our community until it reaches adulthood, or placed with an appropriate foster family in the Colony."

"And what does Dani want?"

The woman's heart rate began to speed up. "She wants the best future for the child."

"I want to hear it from her."

Oh, her heart was racing now. "She does not wish to see you."

Fang knew she was lying, but he didn't want to call her on it. Not yet. "What if I don't care? What if I want not only my child, but the mother released to me to care for it?"

"Dandelion has contractual responsibilities to the Colony, which include bearing a certain number of children to ensure the sustainability of the population."

Wasn't that what the incubus had wanted her for? That night in the clinic, when he'd kidnapped her, Dani had said the incubus had wanted her as a breeder to bear his babies. Only his.

Well, that was never going to happen.

"What would it cost to have her contractual responsibilities transferred to me? So that she bears children for me, instead of the Colony?"

Relief flooded her expression for a moment, before she smoothed it back into a blank mask. "That will be…quite costly, Dr Fang. And practically impossible, in this case, as the final negotiations are almost complete. Another party has already purchased Dandelion's contract. We do, however, have a selection of other nubile girls who might suit your needs, many of which are as yet untouched. Especially if you mean to claim this child, which Dandelion's buyer has no interest in keeping."

Everything Dani had said was true.

Stars, he should have come sooner.

"That is unacceptable. Dani is mine. How much for her contract?"

Up went her heart rate again, but it was excitement, not fear accelerating it now. The woman smelled victory. "I'm afraid the buyer will not sell."

As if Dani could be bought or sold. People could not be purchased. "How much?"

"You must understand, our negotiations are of a confidential nature. I couldn't possibly…"

"Who is he, and how much is he paying for her?"

TWENTY-SIX

"Dandelion, report to the medical room for a health check," Donna said.

Dani looked down at her dinner. She hadn't been able to keep anything down all day – this was the first time she'd actually felt like eating. "Can't I finish my dinner first?"

"You may eat it on the way." Donna

turned and marched off, evidently expecting Dani to follow.

Sighing, Dani bit into her ration bar and hurried to catch up. She'd already had her standard health check for the week. This one must be because of the baby.

"Will the scanner be able to check the baby's health yet? Will I be able to see it?" Dani asked eagerly. "How frequently will I need health checks, now I'm pregnant?" She'd never stripped out of her clothes so fast. She didn't even care how cold the examination table was beneath her back, if it meant she could actually see her baby.

"That will be up to your new owner. He will assume responsibility for your health now, pending this final health check before the contracts are signed."

Her health…but not the baby's. Oh God, it was too late. Donna had sold her contract to Shade, and they were going to force her to have an abortion.

"No, you can't. This is Fang's baby, too. He should have a say in this. Stop. You can't do this!" Dani struggled to get up from the examination table, but Donna shoved her down.

The sting of something sharp touched her neck, before everything went dark.

TWENTY-SEVEN

Dani woke with a start. The cold examination table was still beneath her back, but the hands on her shoulders had not been there before.

"Hold still for your health scan, or I will have to start again."

That was Fang's voice. Her eyes flew open. Sure enough, he was there, holding the scanner. Like he was a doctor, not a dentist.

"Fang, you have to help me. Donna's sold my contract to Shade. You have to say you've seen something terrible in my health scan. A…horrible disease he could catch from me, that will burn his dick off. Or an alien fungus growing in my teeth that makes my breath poisonous to anyone in a ten metre radius. Or…" Damn it, she couldn't think of anything else. "Something the scanner won't pick up, so she won't be able to check it, and say you'll have to take me to the hospital for further tests or treatment or something."

Fang just chuckled. Like this was a joke. "Don't worry, everything will be fine."

"But it won't – " Dani began, only to close her mouth when Donna entered the room.

"And what is your assessment?" Donna asked. "Is the girl healthy?"

"In perfect health," Fang said. Traitor.

"Sign here, please." Donna thrust her tablet at Fang, who signed the report like he didn't care that he was signing Dani's life away.

Liar. He didn't love her. He didn't even look back at her. He just left.

"There. Now it's official. You're no longer a resident of Star Farm. Your contract belongs to your new owner now. Your body belongs to him for the next ten years, or four live births, as agreed in your original contract. Any children you bear belong to him from conception right through to adulthood, as you waived any rights to motherhood in your initial contract. You will obey him in all things, or he will punish you as he sees fit. If he is displeased with his purchase, he will return for a refund, and Star Farm can't afford that. The money from selling your contract will buy us farming land on Elysium, with an orchard and full complement of livestock, where you may join us when your contract is finished. If you displease him and we have to return the fee he paid, I will make sure every girl here knows you are the one responsible for us losing the farm we've waited so long for. Do you understand? This isn't just about you. This is about all of us."

Dani swallowed. Star Farm was a

collective. Everything they did was for the good of everyone, always. Working together to build a better world for them and their children. "I understand."

"You will be a willing, obedient, hardworking mother to his children."

"Yes, I will." Dani touched her belly. "And…this baby? Will I be allowed to…?"

"The father has agreed to take responsibility for the upkeep of your child, so if you carry it to term, the baby will belong to him."

Dani breathed a sigh of relief. So that's what Fang had meant. He'd saved their baby, and he'd take care of it. So that in ten years' time, maybe she'd be allowed to see them again.

"Thank you, Donna." she said.

"I do what I do for the good of the Colony," Donna said.

Of course. "As do we all."

Then a sharp sting at her neck dropped her into the darkness again.

TWENTY-EIGHT

The next time Dani woke, she knew instantly she wasn't on the examination table, even if she was still naked. She was lying on sheets that were softer than anything she'd ever slept on before. She shouldn't be so surprised, she told herself. She was probably in her owner's bed. A man who could afford to buy people, or farms on pristine planets, would only sleep on the very best.

So why on Earth or any other planet did he want a nobody like her?

"Hello?" she called.

No answer.

She called again, and when no one seemed to care, she rose from the bed, wrapping the sheet around her to cover her nakedness, as she explored her new home. It appeared to be an entire house, laid out in one enormous, circular room. A huge bed occupied a platform higher than the rest of it, almost like a stage. Dani shivered. Having sex with a stranger she had to obey was bad enough, but if there was an audience of people watching…

She swallowed. She was doing this for

the farm on Elysium. She had to remember that.

A blinking red light drew her attention. She crept closer.

The light came from a small device, with a piece of paper stuck to it. On the paper, someone had scrawled: PRESS BUTTON WHEN AWAKE.

Dani lifted up the paper. It was the red button that was flashing. She could wait, and enjoy the last few moments of relative freedom, alone, or she could press the button and find out what Shade expected her to do first.

She'd never shied away from doing what was necessary before, so Dani didn't hesitate. She mashed the button.

Nothing happened for several long minutes, until a slight hiss came from behind her. Dani whipped around.

Fang stepped into the room. "You're awake."

Fury welled up inside her. "You're a traitor. You're working for that arsehole. You have been all along. How much did Shade pay you?"

"Who?" Fang looked blank. "Oh, that shifty incubus from the Cantina. No, I work for myself at the clinic. I own the clinic."

"But Shade bought me," Dani said slowly.

Fang laughed. "That's who the other party was? Figures. No wonder her price was so low. I mean, I've heard of virginity auctions go for ten times that, and this was for so much more. I thought I'd have to sell a few of my ships at least, but nope. She did clean me out of my cash reserves, so I'm afraid we might have to go without a few luxuries until next month's rents come in, or if by some miracle the Colony government actually pays the clinic fees on time, instead of late like they usually do, but I'm sure we'll manage."

"I don't understand," Dani whispered. "You're my new owner?"

"Stars, no. You can't own people. It was declared illegal on Earth centuries ago, and it's never been legal in the Titan system or this one. I am, however, the new owner of the contract of somewhat questionable legality that you signed back on Earth."

She wasn't sure whether to laugh or cry. "But I have to obey you. Do whatever you say. For ten years or four babies, so you don't send me back and demand a refund, and they'll lose the Farm."

Fang's eyes narrowed. "Funny, I was told no refunds. Once I'd signed the contract, the transaction was final, and I couldn't send you back. As if I'd ever want to." His gaze wandered down her body, and his eyes widened. "Stars, why are you still naked? There are clothes in the cupboard there. Did none of them fit?"

Dani glanced over to the place he was pointing at. There was another paper square stuck to the wall panel that said SOME CLOTHES FOR YOU. I HOPE THEY FIT.

"I'm a little strapped for cash right

now, like I told you, but if you need more, I'm sure we can afford a few things. Next month, you can commission a whole wardrobe from whoever you want, as long as you're willing to wait that long."

Dani slid open the cupboard door. A rainbow of fabric greeted her. She pulled out the nearest item — a dress in shimmery shades of blue, from the palest aqua to the deepest midnight, like someone had captured the ocean and printed it on a dress. It was shaped like the utilitarian shifts she'd worn on the Farm, but that's where the similarities ended. The fabric of this dress slid through her fingers like it was liquid.

"It's synthsilk," Fang said quickly. "Almost identical to real silk, except it's synthetic and not organic. There's a shop in the city that makes clothing and other textiles with it in the most amazing colours. Every time I walked past it, I imagined what you would look like wearing whatever was in the window. So when I had to get you some clothing quickly, that's where I went." He looked anxious. "If you don't like it, I promise you can take it all back and buy something you do like next month. Anything you want."

Dani sat down on the bed, absently stroking the dress. "But why? You own me."

He pointed to the spot beside her. "Can I sit?" When she nodded, he did. "I don't own you, Dani. No one owns you but yourself. I bought your contract so they couldn't control you any more. You asked for my help. This seemed like the best way."

"But why? I'm nobody. My contract must have cost you a fortune. I can't repay you for that. I already owe you…ten years and…children…" Tears spilled down her cheeks and she couldn't stop them.

Fang dropped to his knees before her. "Dani, look at me, please. You don't owe me anything. I did this for us and for our child."

"But you could have picked anyone! Why me?"

"How much do you know about vampires?"

Dani blinked. She had to think for a moment, before she finally said, "Well, you bite people. Inject them with venom that relaxes them and dulls pain, and you drink blood. Not much, and you can drink other things, too. Like in the Cantina that night. And you're amazing at sex." She felt her face redden.

He nodded. "Do you know how new vampires are made?"

She'd seen a lot of films back on Earth, but they were fiction. The only real vampire she'd met was Fang. "Maybe you need to bite them?" she suggested uncertainly.

"Well, it starts with a bite. Three, actually, according to the collected knowledge of my kind."

He'd bitten her way more than three times. Dani paled. "You mean I'm a vampire now?"

He shook his head. "No, of course not. You're as Human now as you were on the night we met. Which is why this is all so strange. You see, the biting bit only works if the couple are mates. I know it sounds all magical and mystical, but it's more about genetic compatibility. When two mates find each other, and one bites the other, their mate's blood makes them…high. That's how they know they're mates. And after three bites, it's like those fertility shots they were handing out at the Cantina. Vampire children are very rare, and very precious, which only paired mates can even conceive, and even then, it's rare for them to have more than one child. My parents were mated for fifty years, and I'm an only child. So when I bit you and your blood went straight to my head, and then you said you were pregnant…"

Dani blew out a breath. "You think I'm your fated mate."

"I don't just think that. I know. Which is why I'd do anything, give anything, to keep you and our child safe." He closed his eyes and blew out a frustrated breath. "I thought it was a vampire thing. I never thought I'd have a mate, let alone one who was Human. Usually, we have a mating ceremony, like a marriage, only a bit more binding. I won't ask you to do that – not ever, if you don't want to. But when I look at you, I think of forever, which is something I'd never considered before." He opened his eyes, then frowned. "Look, is there any chance you could put that dress on? It's really hard to concentrate on serious things when you're sitting there all naked and sexy on my bed and all I can think about is how beautiful you'd look lying naked on my bed, with your legs spread wide just for me, and my hands stroking you exactly the way you like best."

If she closed her eyes, she could almost feel his hand, stroking her. She wanted that, maybe just as much as he did. Maybe…

Dani held up her hands. "For the stupid farm girl in the room, can we just get a few things straight? Our baby is safe." He nodded. "I'm safe." Another nod. "The only person who can control me or tell me what to do is you, because you bought my contract from FarmStars." He looked like he wanted to protest, so Dani rushed to continue, "But you don't want to control me. The one thing you want most right now is to have sex with me, in your bed, right now." That got a nod and a smile. "I can't think of a better way to celebrate. Can you?"

Within moments, she was lying naked on his bed, his hands parting her thighs, as he proceeded to stroke her with everything he had. First his hands, followed by his tongue, until finally, he stroked her deep inside with his rock hard cock and nothing else in the universe mattered but the two of them.

TWENTY-NINE

They made love all day, until Dani fell asleep in Fang's arms. All in all, it was the best day of his life. Until she woke up, wanting to know what was involved in a vampire mating ceremony, and within the hour they were kneeling before Coven Leader Lavinia, with his fangs at Dani's throat, praying to any deity who would listen that he could make it back to bed with Dani before his cock exploded early.

Somehow, he managed it, and he'd barely thrust all the way inside her before she cried out in pleasure, too. Almost like magic. Maybe there was something in this fated mates thing, after all.

They consummated their mating no less than six times that night, maybe more – for with Dani in his arms, he was far too busy to count.

It was more than a week before Fang could drag his thoughts or his hands away from Dani, and when he did, they didn't stray far.

He decided to call Claw.

"Hey, you remember when you asked me if I'd done anything illegal?" Fang asked.

"Yeah," came the cautious response.

"What if I think I've signed an illegal contract?" Because the more he looked at it, the more suspicious he became of Star Farm.

Silence for a long moment, then, "You'd better let me take a look at it."

Fang hit send.

"Stars. We need to tell Talon about this, before he does something stupid."

Fang's heart sank. "Why? Where is he?"

"At Star Farm."

ABOUT THE AUTHOR

Demelza Carlton has always loved the ocean, but on her first snorkelling trip she found she was afraid of fish.

She has since swum with sea lions, sharks and sea cucumbers and stood on spray drenched cliffs over a seething sea as a seven-metre cyclonic swell surged in, shattering a shipwreck below.

Demelza now lives in Perth, Western Australia, the shark attack capital of the world.

The *Ocean's Gift* series was her first foray into fiction, followed by her suspense thriller *Nightmares* trilogy. She swears the *Mel Goes to Hell* series ambushed her on a crowded train and wouldn't leave her alone.

Want to know more? You can follow Demelza on Facebook, Twitter, YouTube or her website, Demelza Carlton's Place at:

www.demelzacarlton.com

More Books by Demelza Carlton

<u>Colony: Holiday series</u>

Cowboys and Aliens (#1)

Ghost (#2)

Vulcan (#3)

Cupid (#4)

Valentine(#5)

Prometheus (#6)

<u>**Colony: Aqua series**</u>

Halcyon (#1)

Poseidon (#2)

Apollo (#3)

<u>**Colony: Nyx series**</u>

Fang (#1)

Talon (#2)

Claw (#3)

<u>**Siren of War series**</u>

Ocean's Justice (#1)

Ocean's Widow (#2)

Ocean's Bride (#3)

Ocean's Rise (#4)

Ocean's War (#5)

How To Catch Crabs

<u>**Nightmares Trilogy**</u>

<u>**Romance a Medieval Fairytale series**</u>

Enchant: Beauty and the Beast Retold

Dance: Cinderella Retold

Fly: Goose Girl Retold

Revel: Twelve Dancing Princesses
Retold

Silence: Little Mermaid Retold

Awaken: Sleeping Beauty Retold

Embellish: Brave Little Tailor Retold

Appease: Princess and the Pea Retold

Blow: Three Little Pigs Retold

Return: Hansel and Gretel Retold

Wish: Aladdin Retold

Melt: Snow Queen Retold

Spin: Rumpelstiltskin Retold

Kiss: Frog Prince Retold

Reflect: Snow White Retold

Roar: Goldilocks Retold

Cobble: Elves and the Shoemaker Retold

Float: Enchanted Horse Retold

Steal: Forty Thieves Retold

Call: Pied Piper Retold

Fall: Scheherazade Retold

Feather: Swan Maidens Retold

Cross: Billy Goats Gruff Retold

Weave: Rapunzel Retold

Claim: Puss in Boots Retold

Curse: Rose Red Retold

Cross: Three Billy Goats Gruff Retold

Weave: Rapunzel Retold

Claim: Puss in Boots Retold

<u>**Heart of Stone series**</u>

Heart of Steel (#0)

Broken Chains (#1)

Broken Bonds (#2)

Broken Dreams (#3)

<u>**Heart of Steel series**</u>

Heart of Steel (#0)

Stone Guardian (#1)

Stone Champion (#2)

Stone Sentinel (#3)

Stone Shadow (#4)

www.ingramcontent.com/pod-product-compliance
Lightning Source LLC
Chambersburg PA
CBHW070311190726
48291CB00012B/1073